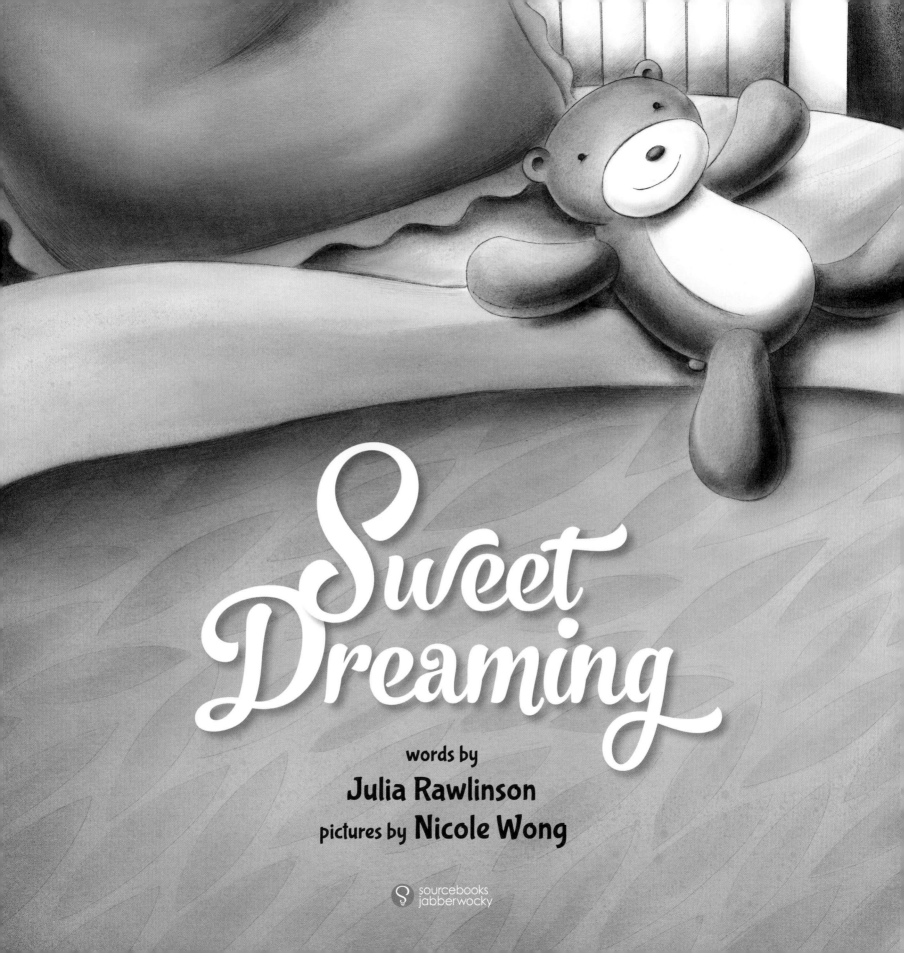

Sweet Dreaming

words by
Julia Rawlinson

pictures by **Nicole Wong**

sourcebooks
jabberwocky

"I can't sleep!" said Molly.

"You can," said her mom.

"Just think of a story and sleep will soon come.

Pretend you're a bird in the sun-dazzled sky,
looping the loop as the wind rushes by.
You're swooping through sunbeams
and skimming the trees."

"I like being a bird," Molly murmured, "but, please,
could we not have so much of the swooping and skimming?"

"Okay," said her mom. "Be…

a penguin who's swimming

through icy-cold waters and sliding through snow,

to an Antarctic party where penguins all go

to dance waltzes and polkas and dine on fresh fish."

"That sounds great," Molly shivered, "but really I wish that you could have pretended me somewhere less chilly."

"You're right," said her mom. "The Antarctic was silly. Don't worry. You're still in your warm, cozy bed. Close your eyes and pretend you're…

a camel instead.

The camel is swishing through soft, golden sand,

where an African sun bakes the dry desert land.

The heat makes you sleepy. Your heavy eyes blink…"

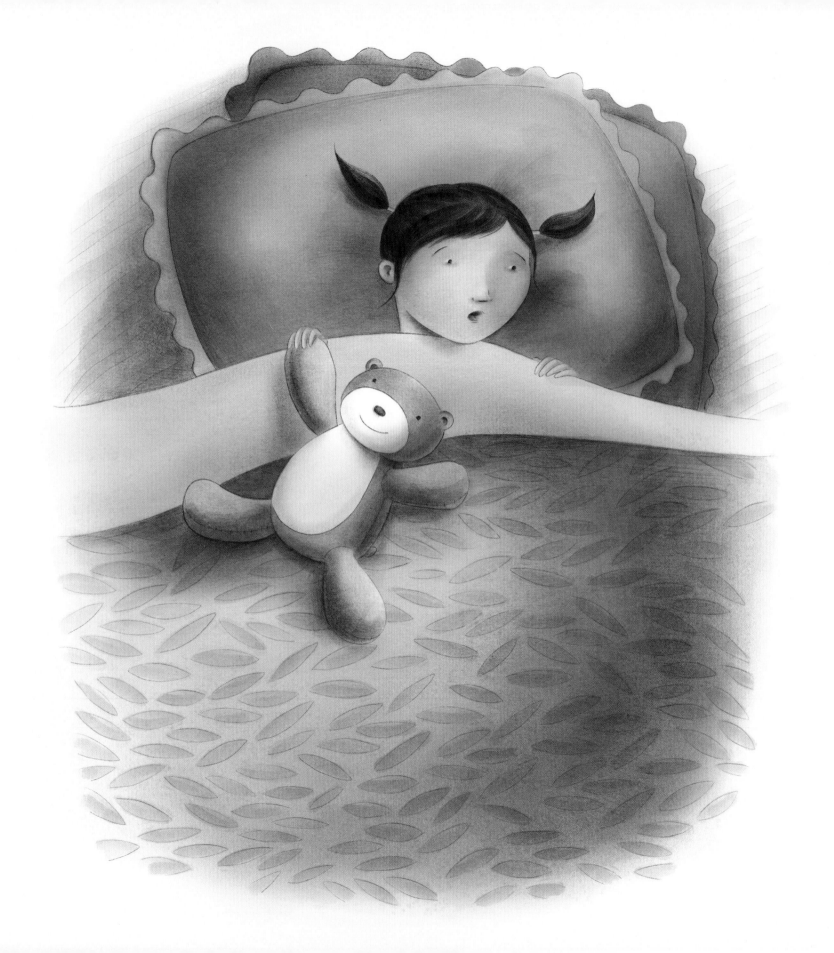

"Camel's thirsty," said Mol. "Could it please have a drink?"

"I'll fetch it some water," said Mom with a sigh.

"And then we'll pretend that you're somewhere less dry…

in a little boat rocked by a sleepy sea swell."

"Oh, I know!" Molly cried…

"Let's have pirates as well,
with monkeys and parrots
and treasure and fighting."

"No pirates," said Mom. "They are much too exciting.

You'll never be sleepy with pirates at play…

So let's wish up a whale,

who can whoosh you away…

and carry you safe to a tropical land,

where you lie down to sleep on the shimmering sand.

The palm leaves above softly sway in the breeze."

"This is good." Molly yawned.

"Will you tell me more, please?"

But Mom's eyes were closed. She was sleeping already,

so Mol tucked her in with her second-best teddy,

and snuggled back down to the sound of soft breathing,

and drifted away to…

the world of sweet dreaming,

where waves sparkled bright in the glimmering light

of a sliver of moon that sailed on through the night.

And Molly's imaginings danced hand in hand,

to the song of the sea on the silvery sand.

To Lucy, who lived stories with me —J. R.

To Bella and Colin —N. W.

Published by Sourcebooks Jabberwocky, an imprint of Sourcebooks, Inc.
P.O. Box 4410, Naperville, Illinois 60567-4410
(630) 961-3900
Fax: (630) 961-2168
sourcebooks.com

Library of Congress Cataloging-in-Publication Data

Names: Rawlinson, Julia, author. | Wong, Nicole (Nicole E.), illustrator.
Title: Sweet dreaming / Julia Rawlinson, Nicole Wong.
Description: Naperville, Illinois : Sourcebooks Jabberwocky, [2018] |
    Summary: Molly's mother imagines stories to lull her to sleep, from
    swooping birds to a quiet beach, and soon one of them has nodded off.
Identifiers: LCCN 2016058179 | (13 : alk. paper)
Subjects: | CYAC: Bedtime—Fiction. | Mother and child—Fiction. |
    Imagination—Fiction.
Classification: LCC PZ7.R1974 Iaf 2018 | DDC [E]—dc23 LC record available
at https://lccn.loc.gov/2016058179

Source of Production: Leo Paper, Heshan City, Guangdong Province, China
Date of Production: April 2018
Run Number: 5011754

Printed and bound in China.
LEO 10 9 8 7 6 5 4 3 2 1